A Peter Rabbit Tale

Peter Rabbit

Based on the original story by
Beatrix Potter
with all new illustrations

Cover illustration by
Anita Nelson
Book illustrations by
Pat Schoonover

Publications International, Ltd.

Once there were four little bunnies named Flopsy, Mopsy, Cottontail, and Peter. They lived with their mother under a big fir tree. One day, Mother Rabbit said, "You may go and play, but stay out of Mr. McGregor's garden. He does not like rabbits."

So Flopsy, Mopsy, and Cottontail went to find wild blackberries. Peter thought he looked fine in his new blue jacket with the shiny brass buttons. Mother Rabbit set off to buy brown bread and buns.

Flopsy, Mopsy, and Cottontail were good little bunnies. They always listened to their mother. They went down the lane to look for black-berries.

But Peter was a naughty rabbit. He ran down the lane, through the fields, and squeezed under the gate to Mr. McGregor's garden! He could hardly wait to nibble some crunchy radishes and carrots.

First, Peter ate some lettuce and green beans. Then he ate some radishes. The carrots were delicious, but the onions were too strong. When Peter's tummy began to ache he looked for some parsley.

But at the end of a garden row Peter saw Mr. McGregor. When Mr. McGregor saw Peter Rabbit, he jumped up, grabbed his rake, and chased after the scared little bunny. "Stop, thief!" shouted Mr. McGregor.

Peter was very frightened. He ran through the garden looking for the gate. Where was it? Poor Peter lost one shoe among the cabbages and the other in the potato patch. Without his shoes he could run much faster. He might have gotten away, but the shiny brass buttons on his new blue jacket tangled in a gooseberry net!

The only way Peter could get free was to wriggle out of his new blue jacket and leave it behind. Peter cried. He would never get back home!

Peter had no time to feel sorry for himself. Mr. McGregor was not far behind. Hop! Jump! Peter rushed into a tool shed and jumped inside a watering can. It would have been a good place to hide, if it were not half-full of water.

Mr. McGregor was sure Peter was hiding in the shed. Carefully he began turning over flower pots, looking for the naughty little rabbit. Then Peter sneezed, "Kertyschoo!" And Mr. McGregor was after him again.

Peter leaped out the window, upsetting three flower pots. Mr. McGregor tried to follow him, but the window was too small. And Mr. McGregor was tired, so he went back to his work in the garden.

Peter was shaking with fear and out of breath. He was also very damp from sitting in that watering can. After a while, he began to wander around, going hippity-hop, not very fast. He saw a door in the wall, but it was locked.

Just then, a little mouse scampered past him. Peter asked her the way to the gate, but she had a large pea in her mouth and could not answer. Peter began to cry again.

Peter wandered to a fish pond. There, a white cat sat staring at the goldfish swimming in the pond. Peter had been warned about cats; he decided not to ask her the way to the gate.

Suddenly, close to him, he heard the noise of a hoe—scritch, scratch, scratch, scritch.

Peter hid underneath some bushes. Nothing happened. So he climbed into a wheelbarrow for a better look. The first thing he saw was Mr. McGregor hoeing onions. He had his back to Peter.

Just across the garden, beyond Mr. McGregor, was the gate! Peter ran to the gate as fast as he could and slid under it to safety. Mr. McGregor could not catch him now!

Peter did not stop running until he reached his home beneath the big fir tree.

Mother Rabbit was busy cooking. Flopsy, Mopsy, and Cottontail were eating bread, milk, and blackberries. Peter was too tired to eat. His mother tucked him into his bed and gave him a dose of chamomile tea. Mother Rabbit wondered where he had lost his shoes and his new jacket with the brass buttons.

Only Mr. McGregor knew where Peter's clothes were. He had hung them up like a scarecrow to frighten the blackbirds away from his garden.